CW01024004

This edition published by Parragon Books Ltd in 2015

Parragon Books Ltd
Chartist House
15–17 Trim Street
Bath BA1 1HA, UK
www.parragon.com

Illustrated by Annabelle Ozanne
Edited by Grace Harvey
Designed by Kathryn Davies
Production by Charlotte McKillop

ISBN 978-1-4723-7915-3

Printed in China

A COLLECTION OF
NURSERY RHYMES

Bath • New York • Cologne • Melbourne • Delhi
Hong Kong • Shenzhen • Singapore • Amsterdam

Contents

Action Rhymes

Animal Rhymes

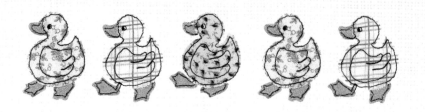

Counting Rhymes

Bedtime Rhymes

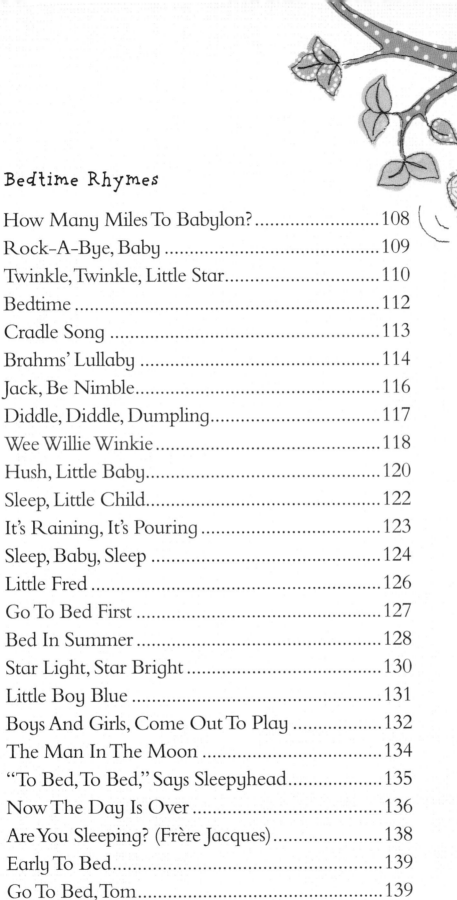

This Little Piggy

This little piggy went to market,
(wiggle child's big toe)

This little piggy stayed at home,
(wiggle child's second toe)

This little piggy had roast beef,
(wiggle child's middle toe)

This little piggy had none.
(wiggle child's fourth toe)

And this little piggy went...
(wiggle child's little toe)

"Wee, wee, wee," all the way home.
(tickle child's foot)

Row, Row, Row Your Boat

(mime rowing motion throughout)

Row, row, row your boat
Gently down the stream.
Merrily, merrily, merrily, merrily,
Life is but a dream!

Humpty Dumpty

Humpty Dumpty sat on a wall,
(mime rocking back and forth)

Humpty Dumpty had a great fall.
(mime falling)

All the King's horses and all the King's men
(mime being on a horse)

Couldn't put Humpty together again.
(mime sadness)

The Grand Old Duke Of York

(every time you say the word "up" stand up, and every time you say the word "down" sit down)

Oh, the grand old Duke of York,
He had ten thousand men,
He marched them up to the top of the hill,
And he marched them down again.

When they were up, they were up.
And when they were down, they were down.
And when they were only halfway up,
They were neither up nor down.

Little Miss Muffet

Little Miss Muffet
Sat on a tuffet,
Eating her curds and whey.
(mime eating from a bowl)

Along came a spider,
Who sat down beside her
And frightened Miss Muffet away.
(walk fingers and mime being scared)

I'm A
Little Teapot

I'm a little teapot, short and stout,
Here's my handle, here's my spout.
*(place one hand on your hip and hold
other arm out with elbow and wrist bent)*

When I get my steam up, hear me shout,
Tip me up and pour me out!
(lean over as if you're pouring out the tea)

The Wheels On The Bus

The wheels on the bus go
Round and round,
(move hands in a circular motion)
Round and round,
Round and round.
The wheels on the bus go
Round and round,
All day long!

The wipers on the bus go
Swish, swish, swish,
(move hands from side to side)
Swish, swish, swish,
Swish, swish, swish.
The wipers on the bus go
Swish, swish, swish,
All day long!

The people on the bus go
Chat, chat, chat,
(make a beak shape with your hand, then open and close it)
Chat, chat, chat,
Chat, chat, chat.
The people on the bus go
Chat, chat, chat,
All day long!

The horn on the bus goes
Beep, beep, beep,
(mime pressing a horn)
Beep, beep, beep,
Beep, beep, beep.
The horn on the bus goes
Beep, beep, beep,
All day long!

I Hear Thunder

(wiggle fingers to mime rain for first verse)

I hear thunder, I hear thunder.
Hark, don't you? Hark, don't you?
Pitter, patter, raindrops,
Pitter, patter, raindrops,
I'm wet through; so are you.

(open hands to mime sunshine for second verse)

I see blue skies, I see blue skies,
Way up high, way up high!
Hurry up the sunshine,
Hurry up the sunshine,
We'll soon dry! We'll soon dry!

Pat-A-Cake, Pat-A-Cake

Pat-a-cake, pat-a-cake, baker's man.
(clap in rhythm)

Bake me a cake as fast as you can.
(clap in rhythm)

Pat it and roll it and mark it with a "B",
(pat, roll and trace the letter B on palm)

And put it in the oven for baby and me!
(mime putting cake in oven)

This Is The Way

This is the way we wash our hands,
Wash our hands, wash our hands.
This is the way we wash our hands
So early in the morning.

(mime washing hands throughout)

This is the way we brush our teeth,
Brush our teeth, brush our teeth.
This is the way we brush our teeth
So early in the morning.

(mime brushing teeth throughout)

This is the way we wash our face,
Wash our face, wash our face.
This is the way we wash our face
So early in the morning.

(mime washing face throughout)

This is the way we comb our hair,
Comb our hair, comb our hair.
This is the way we comb our hair
So early in the morning.

(mime combing hair throughout)

Round And Round The Garden

Round and round the garden,
Like a teddy bear.

*(draw a circle on child's palm
with your finger)*

One step, two step,
Tickle you under there.

*(walk your fingers up child's arm
and tickle child under the arm)*

Here's The Church

Here's the church,
And here's the steeple.
(interlock fingers; fingers inside, then
raise both index fingers to make a point)

Open the door,
And see all the people.
(turn hands over, keeping fingers interlocked,
then wiggle your fingers)

Miss Polly Had A Dolly

Miss Polly had a dolly who was sick, sick, sick.

(rock arms)

So she called for the doctor to come quick, quick, quick.

(dial and listen)

The doctor came with his bag and his hat,

(hold bag and touch hat)

And he knocked on the door with a rat-a-tat-tat.

(knock on door)

He looked at the dolly and he shook his head,

(shake head)

And he said, "Miss Polly, put her straight to bed!"

(shake finger sternly)

He wrote on a paper for a pill, pill, pill,

(write on paper)

"I'll be back in the morning with the bill, bill, bill."

(wave goodbye)

Incy Wincy Spider

Incy wincy spider
Climbed up the waterspout.
(walk fingers up your child's arm)

Down came the rain
And washed the spider out.
(wiggle fingers to mime rain)

Out came the sun
And dried up all the rain.
(open hands to mime sunshine)

So incy wincy spider
Climbed up the spout again.
(walk fingers up your child's arm)

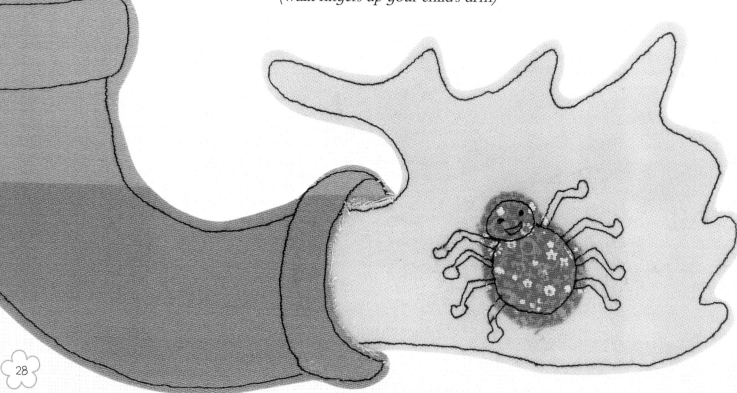

Seesaw, Margery Daw

(mime rocking throughout)

Seesaw, Margery Daw,
Jacky shall have a new master;
Jacky shall earn but a penny a day,
Because he can't work any faster.

Rain, Rain, Go Away

(mime rain falling with fingers throughout)

Rain, rain – go away,
Come again another day.
Little Johnny wants to play.
Rain, rain – go away!

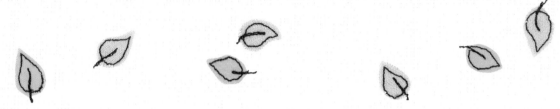

Here We Go Round The Mulberry Bush

(dance around in a circle throughout)

Here we go round the mulberry bush,
The mulberry bush,
The mulberry bush.
Here we go round the mulberry bush
On a cold and frosty morning.

Here we go round the mulberry bush,
The mulberry bush,
The mulberry bush.
Here we go round the mulberry bush
So early in the morning.

Ring-A-Ring O' Roses

Ring-a-ring o' roses,
A pocket full of posies,
(holding hands, go around in a circle)

A-tishoo! A-tishoo!
We all fall down.
(sit down)

Picking up the daisies,
Picking up the daisies,
(pretend to pick flowers)

A-tishoo! A-tishoo!
We all jump up.
(stand up)

Tommy Thumbs

Tommy Thumbs up
And Tommy Thumbs down.

(wiggle thumbs up, then wiggle thumbs down)

Tommy Thumbs dancing
All around town.

(wiggle thumbs)

Dance him on your shoulders,
Dance him on your head.

(tap thumbs on shoulders, then tap thumbs on head)

Dance him on your knees
And tuck him into bed.

(tap thumbs on knees, then hide thumbs in fists)

Jack And Jill

Jack and Jill went up the hill
To fetch a pail of water.

(pretend to walk)

Jack fell down and broke his crown,
And Jill came tumbling after.

(roll arms in a tumbling motion)

Up Jack got, and home did trot,
As fast as he could caper;

(pretend to run)

And went to bed, to mend his head
With vinegar and brown paper.

(mime going to bed)

A Sailor Went To Sea, Sea, Sea

A sailor went to sea, sea, sea,

(make waves with hands)

To see what he could see, see, see,

(raise hand to forehead, and look around)

But all that he could see, see, see,

(raise hand to forehead, and look around)

Was the bottom of the deep, blue sea, sea, sea.

(mime waves with hands)

Hickory, Dickory, Dock

Hickory, dickory, dock,

(swing arm back and forth, like a pendulum)

The mouse ran up the clock.

(run fingers up arm)

The clock struck one,

(clap loudly once)

The mouse ran down,

(run fingers down arm)

Hickory, dickory, dock.

(swing arm back and forth again)

Head, Shoulders, Knees And Toes

(point to the body parts throughout)

Head, shoulders, knees and toes,
Knees and toes.
Head, shoulders, knees and toes,
Knees and toes.
And eyes and ears and mouth and nose,
Head, shoulders, knees and toes,
Knees and toes.

(repeat the verse, faster each time)

Teddy Bear, Teddy Bear

Teddy bear, teddy bear,
Turn around.
(turn around)

Teddy bear, teddy bear,
Touch the ground.
(touch the ground)

Teddy bear, teddy bear,
Show your shoe.
(hold out foot)

Teddy bear, teddy bear,
I love you.
(hug child)

Teddy bear, teddy bear,
Run upstairs.
(climb the stairs)

Teddy bear, teddy bear,
Say your prayers.
(hands in prayer)

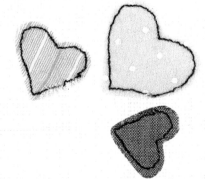

Teddy bear, teddy bear,
Switch out the light.
(blow out candle)

Teddy bear, teddy bear,
Say good night.
(hands as pillow on side of face)

Cock-A-Doodle-Doo

Cock-a-doodle-doo!
My dame has lost her shoe,
My master's lost his fiddlestick,
And knows not what to do.

42

An Elephant walks Like This And That

An elephant walks
Like this and that.

He's terribly tall
And terribly fat.

He has no fingers,
He has no toes.

But goodness gracious,
What a nose!

The Animals Went In Two By Two

The animals went in two by two,
Hoorah! Hoorah!
The animals went in two by two,
Hoorah! Hoorah!

Hey Diddle Diddle

Hey diddle diddle,
The cat and the fiddle,
The cow jumped over the moon.
The little dog laughed
To see such fun,
And the dish ran away with the spoon.

Horsie, Horsie, Don't You Stop

Horsie, horsie, don't you stop,
Just let your feet go clippety-clop.
Your tail goes swish,
And the wheels go round,
Giddy up, we're homeward bound!

Pussy Cat, Pussy Cat

Pussy cat, pussy cat,
Where have you been?

I've been to London
To visit the Queen.

Pussy cat, pussy cat,
What did you do there?

I frightened a little mouse,
Under the chair.

The Owl And The Pussy Cat

The Owl and the Pussy cat went to sea
In a beautiful pea-green boat.
They took some honey, and plenty of money,
Wrapped up in a five-pound note.

The Owl looked up to the stars above,
And sang to a small guitar,
"O, lovely Pussy! O, Pussy, my love,
What a beautiful Pussy you are, you are, you are!
What a beautiful Pussy you are!"

Animal Rhymes

Pussy said to the Owl, "You elegant fowl!
How charmingly sweet you sing!
O, let us be married! Too long we have tarried:
But what shall we do for a ring?"

They sailed away, for a year and a day,
To the land where the Bong-tree grows.
And there in a wood, a Piggy-wig stood
With a ring at the end of his nose, his nose, his nose.
With a ring at the end of his nose.

"Dear Pig, are you willing to sell for one shilling
Your ring?" Said the Piggy, "I will."
So they took it away, and were married next day
By the Turkey who lives on the hill.

They dined on mince, and slices of quince,
Which they ate with a runcible spoon,
And hand in hand, on the edge of the sand,
They danced by the light of the moon, the moon, the moon.
They danced by the light of the moon.

Three Blind Mice

Three blind mice.
Three blind mice.

See how they run.
See how they run.

They all ran after
The farmer's wife,

Who cut off their tails
With a carving knife.

Did you ever see such
A sight in your life,

As three blind mice?

I Had A Little Hobby-Horse

I had a little hobby-horse,
And it was dapple grey.

Its head was made of pea-straw,
Its tail was made of hay.

I sold it to an old woman
For a copper groat,

And I'll not sing my song again
Without a new coat.

Mary Had A Little Lamb

Mary had a little lamb,
His fleece was white as snow,
And everywhere that Mary went,
The lamb was sure to go.

He followed her to school one day,
Which was against the rule.
It made the children laugh and play
To see a lamb at school.

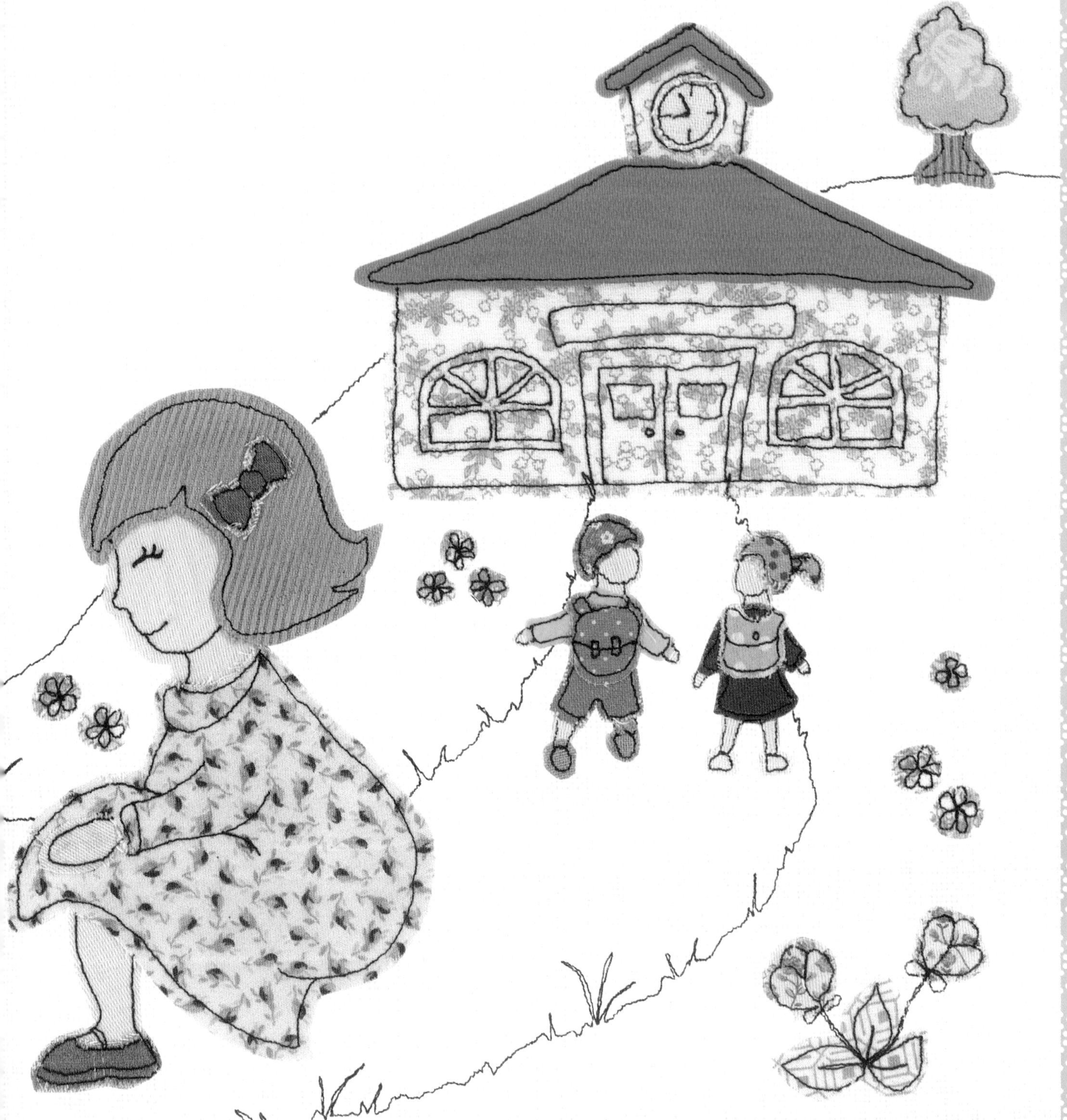

The Lion And The Unicorn

The lion and the unicorn
Were fighting for the crown.

The lion beat the unicorn
All around the town.

Some gave them white bread,
And some gave them brown;

Some gave them plum cake
And drummed them out of town.

Hickety Pickety

Hickety Pickety, my black hen,
She lays eggs for gentlemen,
Sometimes nine, and sometimes ten,
Hickety Pickety, my black hen!

Sing A Song Of Sixpence

Sing a song of sixpence,
A pocket full of rye.
Four and twenty blackbirds,
Baked in a pie.

When the pie was opened,
The birds began to sing;
Wasn't that a dainty dish,
To set before the King?

The King was in his counting house,
Counting out his money;
The Queen was in the parlour,
Eating bread and honey.

The maid was in the garden,
Hanging out the clothes,
When down came a blackbird
And pecked off her nose!

I Had A Little Puppy

I had a little puppy.
His name was Tiny Tim.

I put him in the bathtub,
To see if he could swim.

He drank all the water,
He ate a bar of soap.

The next thing you know,
He had a bubble in his throat.

Once I Saw A Little Bird

Once I saw a little bird
Come hop, hop, hop.

So I cried, "Little bird,
Will you stop, stop, stop?"

And was going to the window
To say, "How do you do?"

But he shook his little tail,
And far away he flew.

There Was An Old Lady Who Swallowed A Fly

There was an old lady who swallowed a fly,
I don't know why she swallowed a fly!

There was an old lady who swallowed a spider,
That wriggled and wiggled and jiggled inside her.
She swallowed the spider to catch the fly;
I don't know why she swallowed a fly!

There was an old lady who swallowed a bird;
How absurd, to swallow a bird!
She swallowed the bird to catch the spider,
She swallowed the spider to catch the fly;
I don't know why she swallowed a fly!

There was an old lady who swallowed a cat;
Fancy that, to swallow a cat!
She swallowed the cat to catch the bird,
She swallowed the bird to catch the spider,
She swallowed the spider to catch the fly;
I don't know why she swallowed a fly!

Animal Rhymes

There was an old lady who swallowed a dog;
What a hog, to swallow a dog!
She swallowed the dog to catch the cat,
She swallowed the cat to catch the bird,
She swallowed the bird to catch the spider,
She swallowed the spider to catch the fly;
I don't know why she swallowed a fly!

There was an old lady who swallowed a cow,
I don't know how she swallowed a cow!
She swallowed the cow to catch the dog,
She swallowed the dog to catch the cat,
She swallowed the cat to catch the bird,
She swallowed the bird to catch the spider,
She swallowed the spider to catch the fly;
I don't know why she swallowed a fly!

There was an old lady who swallowed a horse...
She's dead, of course!

Old Mother Hubbard

Old Mother Hubbard
Went to the cupboard,
To get her poor doggy a bone;
But when she got there,
The cupboard was bare,
And so the poor dog had none.

Higglety, Pigglety, Pop

Higglety, pigglety, pop!
The dog has eaten the mop.
The pig's in a hurry,
The cat's in a flurry,
Higglety, pigglety, pop!

Cackle, Cackle, Mother Goose

Cackle, cackle, Mother Goose,
Have you any feathers loose?
Truly have I, pretty fellow,
Half enough to fill a pillow.
Here are quills, take one or two,
And down to make a bed for you.

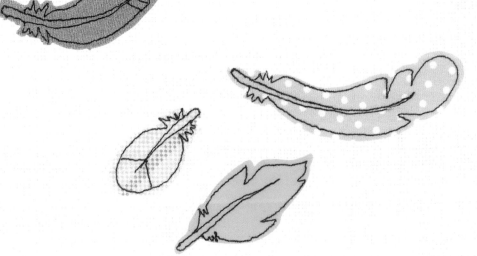

Old MacDonald Had A Farm

Old MacDonald had a farm, E-I-E-I-O!
And on that farm he had some chickens, E-I-E-I-O!
With a cluck-cluck here, and a cluck-cluck there,
Here a cluck, there a cluck, everywhere a cluck-cluck!
Old MacDonald had a farm, E-I-E-I-O!

Old MacDonald had a farm, E-I-E-I-O!
And on that farm he had some sheep, E-I-E-I-O!
With a baa-baa here, and a baa-baa there,
Here a baa, there a baa, everywhere a baa-baa!
Old MacDonald had a farm, E-I-E-I-O!

Old MacDonald had a farm, E-I-E-I-O!
And on that farm he had some cows, E-I-E-I-O!
With a moo-moo here, and a moo-moo there,
Here a moo, there a moo, everywhere a moo-moo!
Old MacDonald had a farm, E-I-E-I-O!

Old MacDonald had a farm, E-I-E-I-O!
And on that farm he had some pigs, E-I-E-I-O!
With an oink–oink here, and an oink–oink there,
Here an oink, there an oink, everywhere an oink–oink!
Old MacDonald had a farm, E-I-E-I-O!

Ding, Dong, Bell

Ding, dong, bell,
Pussy's in the well.

Who put her in?
Little Johnny Flynn.

Who pulled her out?
Little Tommy Stout.

What a naughty boy was that,
To try to drown poor pussy cat,

Who never did him any harm,
But killed all the mice in the farmer's barn!

Little Bo Peep

Little Bo Peep has lost her sheep,
And doesn't know where to find them.
Leave them alone,
And they'll come home,
Wagging their tails behind them.

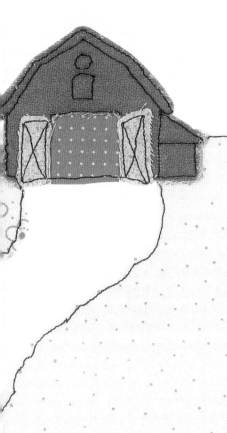

B-I-N-G-O

There was a farmer had a dog,
And Bingo was his name-o.
B-I-N-G-O!
B-I-N-G-O!
B-I-N-G-O!
And Bingo was his name-o!

I Had A Little Hen

I had a little hen, the prettiest ever seen,
She washed up the dishes and kept the house clean.

She went to the mill to fetch us some flour,
And always got home in less than an hour.

She baked me my bread, she brewed me my ale,
She sat by the fire and told a fine tale!

There Was A Crooked Man

There was a crooked man,
And he walked a crooked mile.

He found a crooked sixpence
Upon a crooked stile.

He bought a crooked cat,
Which caught a crooked mouse,

And they all lived together
In a little crooked house.

Three Little Kittens

Three little kittens they lost their mittens,
And they began to cry,
"Oh, Mother dear, we sadly fear,
Our mittens we have lost."
"What! Lost your mittens, you naughty kittens!
Then you shall have no pie."
Meow, meow, meow.
"No, you shall have no pie."

The three little kittens they found their mittens,
And they began to cry,
"Oh, Mother dear, see here, see here,
Our mittens we have found!"
"Put on your mittens, you silly kittens!
And you shall have some pie."
Purr-r, purr-r, purr-r.
"Oh, let us have some pie."

The three little kittens put on their mittens,
And soon ate up the pie,
"Oh, Mother dear, we greatly fear,
That we have soiled our mittens."
"What! Soiled your mittens, you naughty kittens!"
Then they began to sigh,
Meow, meow, meow.
Then they began to sigh.

The three little kittens they washed their mittens,
And hung them out to dry,
"Oh, Mother dear, do you not hear,
Our mittens we have washed."
"What! Washed your mittens, you are good kittens!
But I smell a rat close by."
Meow, meow, meow.
"We smell a rat close by."

Five Little Ducks

Five little ducks went swimming one day,
Over the hill and far away.
Mother duck said, "Quack, quack, quack, quack!"
And only four little ducks came back!

Four little ducks went swimming one day,
Over the hill and far away.
Mother duck said, "Quack, quack, quack, quack!"
And only three little ducks came back!

Three little ducks went swimming one day,
Over the hill and far away.
Mother duck said, "Quack, quack, quack, quack!"
And only two little ducks came back!

Two little ducks went swimming one day,
Over the hill and far away.
Mother duck said, "Quack, quack, quack, quack!"
And only one little duck came back!

One little duck went swimming one day,
Over the hill and far away.
Mother duck said, "Quack, quack, quack, quack!"
And all her five little ducks came back!

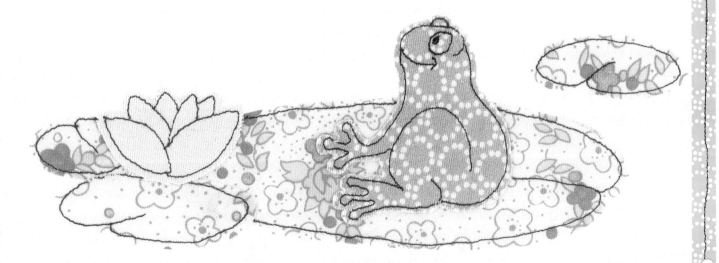

Five Fat Peas

Five fat peas in a pea pod pressed.
One grew, two grew, so did all the rest.
They grew and grew
And did not stop,
Until one day
The pod went POP!

One, Two, Three, Four, Five

One, two, three, four, five,
Once I caught a fish alive,

Six, seven, eight, nine, ten,
Then I let it go again.

Why did you let it go?
Because it bit my finger so.

Which finger did it bite?
This little finger on the right.

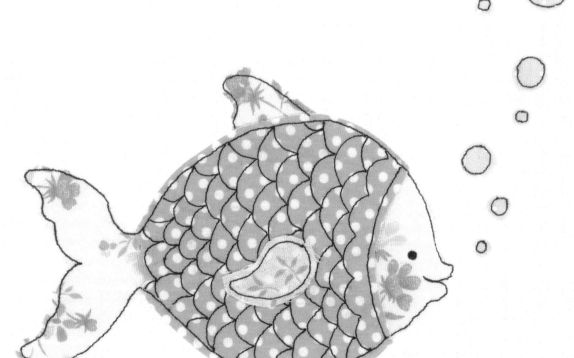

One Man Went To Mow

One man went to mow,
Went to mow a meadow,
One man
And his dog – Woof! –
Went to mow a meadow.

Two men went to mow,
Went to mow a meadow,
Two men, one man
And his dog – Woof! –
Went to mow a meadow.

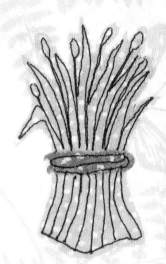

Three men went to mow,
Went to mow a meadow,
Three men, two men, one man
And his dog – Woof! –
Went to mow a meadow.

Four men went to mow,
Went to mow a meadow,
Four men, three men, two men, one man
And his dog - Woof! -
Went to mow a meadow.

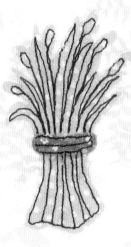

Five men went to mow,
Went to mow a meadow,
Five men, four men, three men, two men, one man
And his dog - Woof! -
Went to mow a meadow.

One For Sorrow

One for sorrow,
Two for joy,
Three for a girl,
Four for a boy,
Five for silver,
Six for gold,
Seven for a secret,
Never to be told.

Five Little Blue Birds

Five little blue birds hopping by my door,
One went to build a nest, and then there were four.

Four little blue birds singing lustily,
One got out of tune, and then there were three.

Three little blue birds and what should one do,
But go in search of dinner, leaving only two.

Two little blue birds singing for fun,
One flew away, and then there was one.

One little blue bird sitting in the sun,
He took a little nap, and then there was none.

Five Little Monkeys Jumping On The Bed

Five little monkeys jumping on the bed.
One fell off and bumped his head;
Mama called the doctor
And the doctor said,
"No more monkeys jumping on the bed."

Four little monkeys jumping on the bed.
One fell off and bumped his head;
Mama called the doctor
And the doctor said,
"No more monkeys jumping on the bed."

Three little monkeys jumping on the bed.
One fell off and bumped his head;
Mama called the doctor
And the doctor said,
"No more monkeys jumping on the bed."

Two little monkeys jumping on the bed.
One fell off and bumped his head;
Mama called the doctor
And the doctor said,
"No more monkeys jumping on the bed."

One little monkey jumping on the bed.
He fell off and bumped his head;
Mama called the doctor
And the doctor said,
"No more monkeys jumping on the bed."

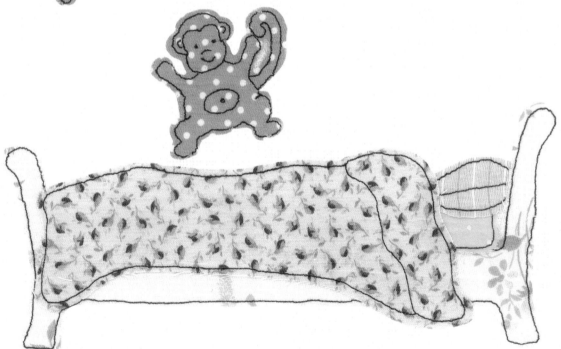

Here Is The Beehive

Here is the beehive.
Where are the bees?
Hidden away where nobody sees.
Watch and you'll see them come out of the hive,
One... two... three... four... five!
Buzz, buzz, buzz, buzz, buzz.

Two Little Dickie Birds

Two little dickie birds,
Sitting on a wall.

One named Peter,
One named Paul.

Fly away, Peter!
Fly away, Paul!

Come back, Peter!
Come back, Paul!

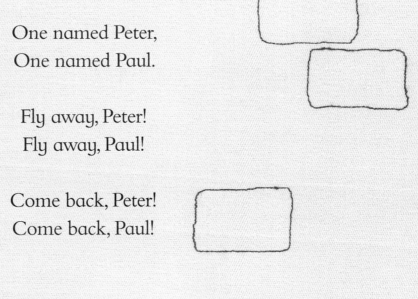

This Old Man

This old man, he played one,
He played knick-knack on my thumb;
With a knick-knack, paddywhack,
Give the dog a bone,
This old man came rolling home.

This old man, he played two,
He played knick-knack on my shoe;
With a knick-knack, paddywhack,
Give the dog a bone,
This old man came rolling home.

This old man, he played three,
He played knick-knack on my knee;
With a knick-knack, paddywhack,
Give the dog a bone,
This old man came rolling home.

Counting Rhymes

This old man, he played four,
He played knick-knack on my door;
With a knick-knack, paddywhack,
Give the dog a bone,
This old man came rolling home.

This old man, he played five,
He played knick-knack on my hive;
With a knick-knack, paddywhack,
Give the dog a bone,
This old man came rolling home.

Rub-A-Dub-Dub

Rub-a-dub-dub,
Three men in a tub,
And who do you think they were?

The butcher, the baker,
The candlestick-maker,
They all sailed out to sea,
'Twas enough to make a man stare.

Five Fat Sausages

Five fat sausages frying in a pan,
All of a sudden, one went BANG!

Four fat sausages frying in a pan,
All of a sudden, one went BANG!

Three fat sausages frying in a pan,
All of a sudden, one went BANG!

Two fat sausages frying in a pan,
All of a sudden, one went BANG!

One fat sausage frying in a pan,
All of a sudden, it went BANG!

Ten Green Bottles

Ten green bottles standing on the wall.
Ten green bottles standing on the wall,
And if one green bottle should accidentally fall,
There'll be...

Nine green bottles standing on the wall.
Nine green bottles standing on the wall,
And if one green bottle should accidentally fall,
There'll be...

Eight green bottles standing on the wall.
Eight green bottles standing on the wall,
And if one green bottle should accidentally fall,
There'll be...

(keep counting down)

Three green bottles standing on the wall.
Three green bottles standing on the wall,
And if one green bottle should accidentally fall,
There'll be...

Two green bottles standing on the wall.
Two green bottles standing on the wall,
And if one green bottle should accidentally fall,
There'll be...

One green bottle standing on the wall.
One green bottle standing on the wall,
And if one green bottle should accidentally fall,
There'll be...

No green bottles standing on the wall.

Hot Cross Buns

Hot cross buns!
Hot cross buns!
One a penny, two a penny,
Hot cross buns!

If you have no daughters,
Give them to your sons.
One a penny, two a penny,
Hot cross buns!

One Little Flower, One Little Bee

One little flower,
One little bee.

One little blue bird
High in the tree.

One little brown bear
Smiling at me.

One is the number I like,
You see!

Five Little Speckled Frogs

Five little speckled frogs,
Sat on a speckled log,
Eating some most delicious bugs.
Yum yum!

One jumped into the pool,
Where it was nice and cool,
Then there were four speckled frogs.
Glug glug!

Four little speckled frogs,
Sat on a speckled log,
Eating some most delicious bugs.
Yum yum!

One jumped into the pool,
Where it was nice and cool,
Then there were three speckled frogs.
Glug glug!

Counting Rhymes

Three little speckled frogs,
Sat on a speckled log,
Eating some most delicious bugs.
Yum yum!

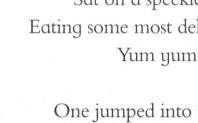

One jumped into the pool,
Where it was nice and cool,
Then there were two speckled frogs.
Glug glug!

Two little speckled frogs,
Sat on a speckled log,
Eating some most delicious bugs.
Yum yum!

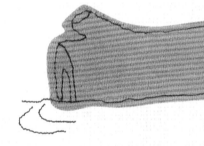

One jumped into the pool,
Where it was nice and cool,
Then there was one speckled frog.
Glug glug!

One little speckled frog,
Sat on a speckled log,
Eating some most delicious bugs.
Yum yum!

He jumped into the pool,
Where it was nice and cool,
Then there were no speckled frogs.
Glug glug!

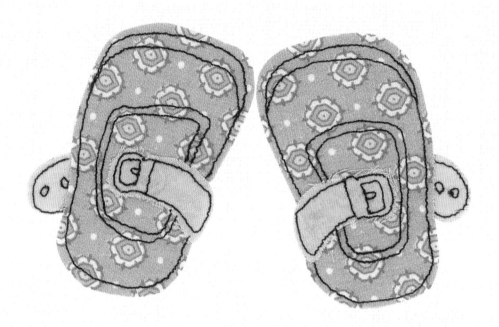

One, Two, Buckle My Shoe

One, two,
Buckle my shoe;

Three, four,
Open the door;

Five, six,
Pick up sticks;

Seven, eight,
Lay them straight;

Nine, ten,
A big, fat hen.

Baa, Baa, Black Sheep

Baa, baa, black sheep,
Have you any wool?

Yes, sir. Yes, sir.
Three bags full.

One for the master,
One for the dame,

And one for the little boy
Who lives down the lane.

Five Currant Buns

Five currant buns in a baker's shop,
Round and fat with a cherry on top.
Along came a boy with a penny one day,
Bought a currant bun and took it away.

Four currant buns in a baker's shop,
Round and fat with a cherry on top.
Along came a girl with a penny one day,
Bought a currant bun and took it away.

Counting Rhymes

Three currant buns in a baker's shop,
Round and fat with a cherry on top.
Along came a boy with a penny one day,
Bought a currant bun and took it away.

Two currant buns in a baker's shop,
Round and fat with a cherry on top.
Along came a girl with a penny one day,
Bought a currant bun and took it away.

One currant bun in a baker's shop,
Round and fat with a cherry on top.
Along came a boy with a penny one day,
Bought the currant bun and took it away.

Five Little Firemen

Five little firemen standing in a row,
1, 2, 3, 4, 5, let's go.
Jump on the engine with a shout,
As quick as a wink, the fire is out.

Four little firemen standing in a row,
1, 2, 3, 4, shh, let's go.
Jump on the engine with a shout,
As quick as a wink, the fire is out.

Three little firemen standing in a row,
1, 2, 3, shh, shh, let's go.
Jump on the engine with a shout,
As quick as a wink, the fire is out.

Two little firemen standing in a row,
1, 2, shh, shh, shh, let's go.
Jump on the engine with a shout,
As quick as a wink, the fire is out.

One little fireman standing in a row,
1, shh, shh, shh, shh, let's go.
Jump on the engine with a shout,
As quick as a wink, the fire is out.

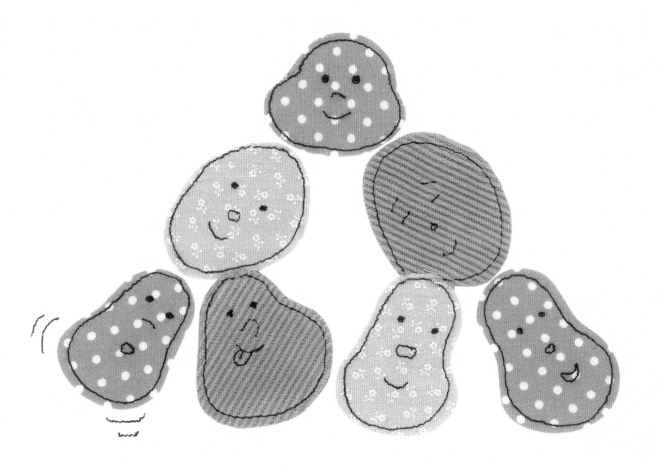

One Potato, Two Potato

One potato,
Two potato,
Three potato, four;

Five potato,
Six potato,
Seven potato, more!

Five Little Monkeys Sitting In A Tree

Five little monkeys sitting in a tree,
Teasing Mister Alligator:
"Can't catch me, can't catch me!"
Along comes Mister Alligator, quiet as can be,
And snapped the monkey out of the tree.

Four little monkeys sitting in a tree,
Teasing Mister Alligator:
"Can't catch me, can't catch me!"
Along comes Mister Alligator, quiet as can be,
And snapped the monkey out of the tree.

Three little monkeys sitting in a tree,
Teasing Mister Alligator:
"Can't catch me, can't catch me!"
Along comes Mister Alligator, quiet as can be,
And snapped the monkey out of the tree.

Two little monkeys sitting in a tree,
Teasing Mister Alligator:
"Can't catch me, can't catch me!"
Along comes Mister Alligator, quiet as can be,
And snapped the monkey out of the tree.

One little monkey sitting in a tree,
Teasing Mister Alligator:
"Can't catch me, can't catch me!"
Along comes Mister Alligator, quiet as can be,
And snapped the monkey out of the tree.

Five Crispy Pancakes

Five crispy pancakes in a frying pan,
Flip them and toss them and catch them if you can.
Along came Garrett for a pancake one day,
Sprinkled it with sugar and took it away.

Four crispy pancakes in a frying pan,
Flip them and toss them and catch them if you can.
Along came 'Nessa for a pancake one day,
Sprinkled it with sugar and took it away.

Three crispy pancakes in a frying pan,
Flip them and toss them and catch them if you can.
Along came Eleanor for a pancake one day,
Sprinkled it with sugar and took it away.

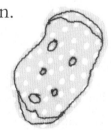

Two crispy pancakes in a frying pan,
Flip them and toss them and catch them if you can.
Along came Lainey for a pancake one day,
Sprinkled it with sugar and took it away.

One crispy pancake in a frying pan,
Flip it and toss it and catch it if you can.
Along came Murphy for a pancake one day,
Sprinkled it with sugar and took it away.

No more pancakes in the frying pan!

One, Two, Three, Four

One, two, three, four,
Mary at the kitchen door:

Five, six, seven, eight,
Eating cherries off a plate.

Ten In The Bed

There were ten in the bed and the little one said,
"Roll over, roll over!"
So they all rolled over and one fell out.

There were nine in the bed and the little one said,
"Roll over, roll over!"
So they all rolled over and one fell out.

There were eight in the bed and the little one said,
"Roll over, roll over!"
So they all rolled over and one fell out.

Counting Rhymes

(keep counting down)

There were three in the bed and the little one said,
"Roll over, roll over!"
So they all rolled over and one fell out.

There were two in the bed and the little one said,
"Roll over, roll over!"
So they all rolled over and one fell out.

There was one in the bed and the little one said,
"Good night!"

How Many Miles To Babylon?

How many miles to Babylon?
Three score and ten.

Can I get there by candle-light?
Yes, and back again.

If your heels are nimble and light,
You may get there by candle-light.

Rock-A-Bye, Baby

Rock-a-bye, baby,
On the tree top,
When the wind blows,
The cradle will rock.

When the bough breaks,
The cradle will fall,
And down will come baby,
Cradle and all.

Twinkle, Twinkle, Little Star

Twinkle, twinkle, little star,
How I wonder what you are!
Up above the world so high,
Like a diamond in the sky.

When the blazing sun is gone,
When he nothing shines upon,
Then you show your little light,
Twinkle, twinkle, all the night.

In the dark blue sky you keep,
And often through my curtains peep,
For you never shut your eye,
Till the sun is in the sky.

Then the traveller in the dark
Thanks you for your tiny spark.
He could not see which way to go,
If you did not twinkle so.

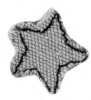

Bedtime

The evening is coming;
The sun sinks to rest.
The crows are all flying
Straight home to the nest.

"Caw," says the crow
As he flies overhead.
"It's time little people
Were going to bed!"

The flowers are closing;
The daisy's asleep.
The primrose is buried
In slumber so deep.

Closed for the night
Are the roses so red.
It's time little people
Were going to bed!

Cradle Song

Golden slumbers kiss your eyes,
Smiles await you when you rise.
Sleep, pretty baby,
Do not cry,
And I will sing a lullaby.

Cares you know not,
Therefore sleep,
While over you a watch I'll keep.
Sleep, pretty darling,
Do not cry,
And I will sing a lullaby.

Brahms' Lullaby

Lullaby, and good night,
With pink roses bedight,
With lilies overspread,
Is my baby's sweet head.

Lay you down now, and rest,
May your slumber be blessed!
Lay you down now, and rest,
May your slumber be blessed!

Lullaby, and good night,
You're your mother's delight,
Shining angels beside
My darling abide.

Soft and warm is your bed,
Close your eyes and rest your head.
Soft and warm is your bed,
Close your eyes and rest your head.

Sleepyhead, close your eyes.
Mother's right here beside you.
I'll protect you from harm,
You will wake in my arms.

Guardian angels are near,
So sleep on, with no fear.
Guardian angels are near,
So sleep on, with no fear.

Lullaby, and sleep tight.
Hush! My darling is sleeping,
On his sheets white as cream,
With his head full of dreams.

When the sky's bright with dawn,
He will wake in the morn.
When noontide warms the world,
He will frolic in the sun.

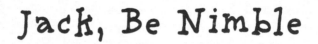

Jack, Be Nimble

Jack, be nimble,
Jack, be quick!

Jack, jump over...
The candlestick!

Diddle, Diddle, Dumpling

Diddle, diddle, dumpling, my son John,
Went to bed with his trousers on;
One shoe off, and the other shoe on,
Diddle, diddle, dumpling, my son John.

Wee Willie Winkie

Wee Willie Winkie
Runs through the town,

Upstairs and downstairs
In his nightgown,

Tapping at the window,
Crying through the lock,

"Are the children all in bed?
It's past eight o'clock!"

Hush, Little Baby

Hush, little baby, don't say a word.
Papa's gonna buy you a mockingbird,

And if that mockingbird won't sing,
Papa's gonna buy you a diamond ring,

And if that diamond ring turns brass,
Papa's gonna buy you a looking-glass,

And if that looking-glass gets broke,
Papa's gonna buy you a billy goat,

And if that billy goat won't pull,
Papa's gonna buy you a cart and bull,

And if that cart and bull turn over,
Papa's gonna buy you a dog named Rover,

And if that dog named Rover won't bark,
Papa's gonna buy you a horse and cart,

And if that horse and cart fall down,
You'll still be the sweetest little baby in town.

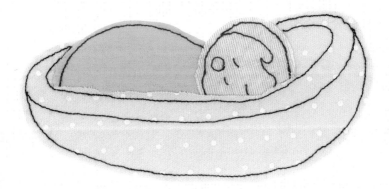

Sleep, Little Child

Sleep, little child, go to sleep,
Mother is here by your bed.
Sleep, little child, go to sleep,
Rest on the pillow your head.

The world is silent and still,
The moon shines bright on the hill,
Then creeps past the windowsill.

Sleep, little child, go to sleep,
Oh, sleep, go to sleep.

It's Raining, It's Pouring

It's raining, it's pouring.
The old man is snoring.
He went to bed and bumped his head,
And he wouldn't get up in the morning.

123

Sleep, Baby, Sleep

Sleep, baby, sleep.
Your father tends the sheep,
Your mother shakes the dreamland tree
And from it fall sweet dreams for thee.
Sleep, baby, sleep,
Sleep, baby, sleep.

Sleep, baby, sleep.
Our cottage vale is deep,
The little lamb is on the green
With snowy fleece so soft and clean.
Sleep, baby, sleep,
Sleep, baby, sleep.

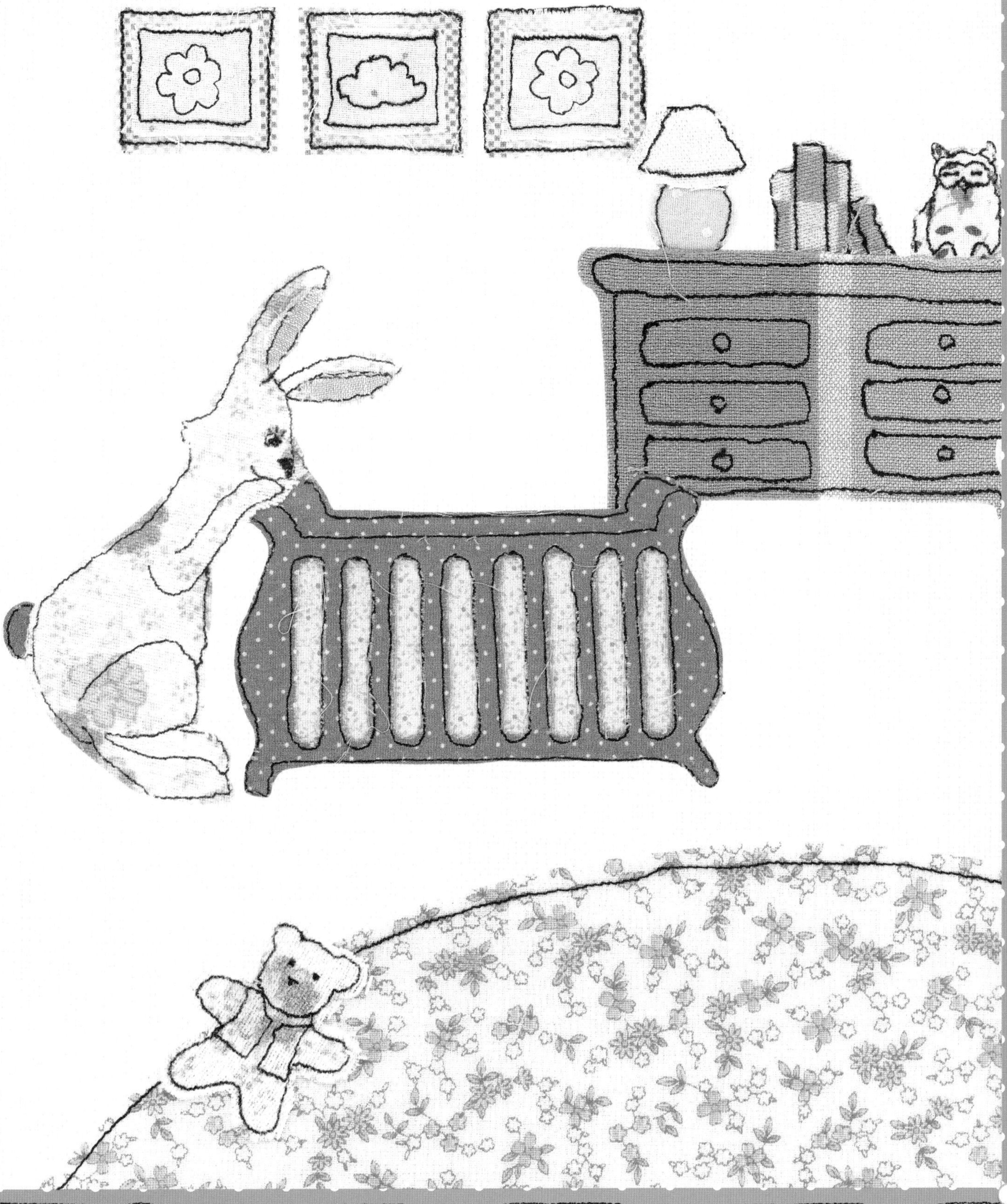

Little Fred

When little Fred went to bed,
He always acted right;
He kissed Mama, and then Papa,
And wished them all good night.

He made no noise, like naughty boys,
But gently upstairs
Directly went, when he was sent,
And always said his prayers.

Go To Bed First

Go to bed first,
A golden purse;

Go to bed second,
A golden pheasant;

Go to bed third,
A golden bird.

Bed In Summer

In winter, I get up at night
And dress by yellow candle-light.
In summer, quite the other way,
I have to go to bed by day.

I have to go to bed and see
The birds still hopping on the tree,
Or hear the grown-up people's feet
Still going past me in the street.

And does it not seem hard to you,
When all the sky is clear and blue,
And I should like so much to play,
To have to go to bed by day?

Star Light, Star Bright

Star light, star bright,
The first star I see tonight;
I wish I may, I wish I might
Have the wish I wish tonight.

Little Boy Blue

Little Boy Blue,
Come blow your horn,
The sheep's in the meadow,
The cow's in the corn.

Where is that boy
Who looks after the sheep?
Under the haystack
Fast asleep.

Will you wake him?
Oh no, not I,
For if I do,
He will surely cry.

Boys And Girls, Come Out To Play

Boys and girls, come out to play,
The moon doth shine as bright as day;

Leave your supper, and leave your sleep,
And come with your playfellows into the street.

Come with a whoop, come with a call,
Come with a good will or not at all.

The Man In The Moon

The man in the moon,
Looked out of the moon,
Looked out of the moon and said:

"It's time for all children on the earth,
To think about getting to bed!"

"To Bed, To Bed," Says Sleepyhead

"To bed! To bed!"
Says Sleepyhead;

"Tarry awhile,"
says Slow;

"Put on the pot,"
Says Greedy-gut.
"We'll sup before we go."

Now The Day Is Over

Now the day is over,
Night is drawing nigh,
Shadows of the evening
Steal across the sky.

Now the darkness gathers,
Stars begin to peep,
Birds and beasts and flowers
Soon will be asleep.

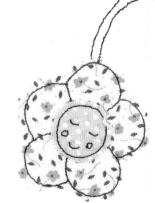

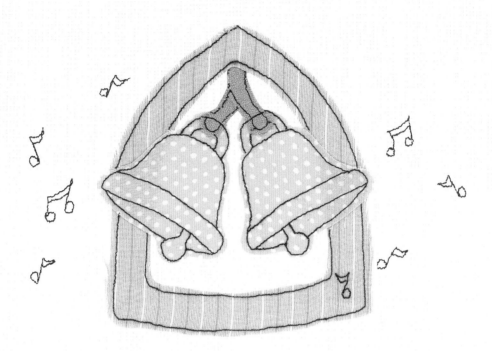

Are You Sleeping?
(Frère Jacques)

Are you sleeping, are you sleeping,
Brother John? Brother John?
Morning bells are ringing, morning bells are ringing!
Ding, dang, dong! Ding, dang, dong!

Frère Jacques, Frère Jacques,
Dormez-vous? Dormez-vous?
Sonnez les matines, sonnez les matines!
Ding, dang, dong! Ding, dang, dong!

Early To Bed

Early to bed,
Early to rise,
Makes my baby
Healthy, wealthy and wise.

Go To Bed, Tom

Go to bed, Tom.
Go to bed, Tom!
Tired or not, Tom,
Go to bed, Tom.

139

Go To Bed Late

Go to bed late,
Stay very small.

Go to bed early,
Grow very tall.

Meet The Artist

Commissioned by Parragon to create unique appliqué artworks for our 'Mother & Baby' range, Annabelle Ozanne, aka Three Red Apples, works from her studio in Devon, England. She makes freehand, machine-embroidered and appliquéd textile illustrations and accessories, using a mix of vintage, recycled and new materials.

Her work has an eclectic, vintage-chic vibe. Annabelle uses a sewing machine to 'draw' straight onto fabric. No fancy tools; she just uses her imagination and a trusty old sewing machine. Her stunning work gives 'Cute as a Button' its stylish and heartwarming look.